Hi!
My name is
Blue.

childhood diabetes.
Keep fighting little ones and hopefully this book
will bring a moment of peace and laughter.

Published by Pen It Publications in the U.S.A.

713-526-3989   www.penitpublications.com

ISBN: 978-1-63984-349-7

Edited by Dina Husseini

Cover Design by Donna Cook, Ryan Douglas

Illustrations by Ryan Douglas

By: Mary Ann Netherton

Illustrated By: Ryan Douglass

I was given that name because I am blue all over, except for my eyes, which are black.

I have eight arms.

Because my arms are so long, I never have trouble grabbing things that are within my reach.

I live in my home
in the ocean.

I am a very happy
Octopus.

My best friend is a Starfish named Carter.

His mom and dad named him that because his grandfather was called Carter too.

Carter is beautiful. He is purple and orange.

His five arms help him walk on the ocean floor. He is really fast.

We play every day.

Carter chases me and then I hide from him.

He counts to ten
then comes out.

Sometimes, I'm hard to see because I blend in with certain parts in the ocean, but Carter always finds me.

Carter once said to me, "Blue, if I had a brother, I'd want him to be just like you."

And, from that day on, I knew that Carter was more than just my best friend.

Even though the two of us look very different, that doesn't stop us from being brothers!

The End...

CPSIA information can be obtained
at www.ICGtesting.com
Printed in the USA
LVHW072033210323
742069LV00045B/1023